SAMURAI JACK

The Seven Labors of Jack

by Tracey West

Based on "Samurai Jack," as created by Genndy Tartakovsky

Scholastic Inc.

New York   Toronto   London   Auckland   Sydney

Mexico City   New Delhi   Hong Kong   Buenos Aires

No part of this publication may be reproduced in whole or in part, or stored in a retrieval system, or transmitted in any form or by any means, electronic, mechanical, photocopying, recording, or otherwise, without written permission of the publisher. For information regarding permission, write to Scholastic Inc., Attention: Permissions Department, 557 Broadway, New York, NY 10012.

ISBN 0-439-40974-8

Cover and interior illustrations by Angel Rodriguez
Designed by Carisa Swenson

12 11 10 9 8 7 6 5 4 3 2 1   3 4 5 6 7 8/0
Printed in the U.S.A.
First printing, February 2003

Samurai Jack walked up another hill. It must have been the fifth hill he had climbed that day, but Jack wasn't counting. He had spent a week walking through this steep country. He barely noticed the hills anymore.

Another person might have whistled a tune to pass the time, or stopped to admire the flowers growing along the trail. But Jack could only focus on one thing: his goal. He had to find a way to travel back through time.

Going back in time was the only way Jack could destroy the evil the powerful demon Aku had brought upon the land. Long ago, after many years of training, Jack had tried using his father's sword of righteousness to stop the wicked Aku from taking over the world.

Because of the sword's might, Aku could not defeat Jack, so he banished him to the future. Jack arrived to find himself in a dangerous future world ruled by Aku. The only way to undo Aku's evil was to go back in time and stop him before he came to power.

Jack's mind was filled with his thoughts, but as a samurai warrior he was always aware of his surroundings. Jack stopped. Something had caught his attention.

For the last three days, the hills had been strangely quiet. There were no birds twittering in the scraggly trees, no small creatures scampering on the ground, not even wind blowing through the tall grasses.

And now Jack had heard something. A sound like a low moan. But was it human?

Jack cautiously made his way toward the noise. As he crossed over the hill, he saw a large boulder jutting out from the hillside. Jack approached, making sure he couldn't be seen.

There was a man on the boulder. His arms and legs were chained to posts embedded in the rock. He wore only a tattered cloak, and his skin was red and cracked from the sun. From the look of his long beard, Jack guessed he had been chained there for quite awhile.

Jack frowned. There was evil in this place after all. He drew his sword and scanned the area. Before he made a move, he had to make sure this wasn't a trap.

Skreeeeeeeeeeee!

The silence was broken again, this time by a piercing cry. Jack looked up. A huge bird circled overhead. It looked like an eagle, but it was made of shimmering metal.

A robot. Jack wasn't surprised. This world was popu-

lated with all kinds of machines and robots. Many of them were designed to keep Aku's evil empire in power.

Suddenly, the bird swooped down from the sky and dove right for the man on the rock. Jack jumped from his hiding place, crying out as he raised his sword.

The eagle perched on the man's chest, digging its claws into his flesh. Its head whipped around at the sound of Jack's yell.

Skreeeeeeeeeeee!

The eagle left the man and raced toward Jack. The samurai stood still and waited. The bird might be fierce, but it wasn't too smart.

Whoosh! Jack's sword moved like lightning through the air as he aimed a blow at the eagle's head.

Then came the sickening sound of metal on metal as the sword sliced off the robot's head in one clean swipe. The bird's heavy body thudded to the dusty ground.

Jack raced to the boulder and used his sword again, this time to cut the chains binding the man to the rock. The man looked at Jack gratefully. "Go . . ." he croaked, his voice cracked with thirst. "Danger."

"Quiet, friend," Jack said. "I will help you."

Jack took a flask of water from his robes and gave the man a long drink. Then he picked up the man in his arms. He had to find a village, or at least some shade.

But before Jack could take a step, a bright green light blinded him. Jack felt the ground slip away beneath his feet, and his ears began to ring. He had the sensation of walking the wrong way into a strong wind.

Then, just as suddenly as it started, the light faded, the air was calm, and all was quiet once more. Jack's feet were on solid ground again, but now he was standing on a smooth marble floor. The man from the rock stood next to him. They seemed to be in some kind of temple, Jack realized. Tall white columns lined the room.

"What is this place?" Jack asked.

"Silence!" a voice boomed.

A bright green face appeared before them. It was a woman's face, as tall as the marble columns. The samurai's mind raced as he tried to figure out what new terror he was facing. A demon? Some kind of projection from a machine? Jack was not sure.

"What gives you the right to free my prisoner?" the woman asked.

"Who are you?" Jack asked.

"I am Divina!" she shouted, her voice bouncing off of the columns. "Now answer me!"

Two bolts of green lightning shot from Divina's eyes. Jack dodged out of the way. Then he moved quickly to defend himself. The samurai jumped toward Divina, his sword raised. The steel blade gleamed as he struck a blow at Divina's face.

A jolting surge of electricity sent Jack flying backward. He tumbled onto the marble floor. His sword still sizzled in his hands.

Divina laughed. "You must be a stranger to these lands, or you would never have tried something so foolish. I will forgive you for that. But I cannot forgive you for helping this criminal."

Jack rose to his feet. Next to him, the man spoke up.

"I am no criminal!" he cried.

Divina ignored him. She kept her eyes fixed on Jack.

"You have freed Theodocus, punished for committing crimes against our civilization," she said. "And now, you shall be punished as well!"

2

Jack could feel Theodocus trembling next to him. But Jack remained calm. He surveyed his surroundings. There had to be some way he could fight Divina. Until he figured out how it wouldn't be wise to make another move.

Divina, meanwhile, seemed to be enjoying herself.

"Let's see," she said. "What will it be? Torn apart by lions? Served to hungry fire ants for supper?"

Divina frowned. "No, no," she said. "They've been done to death. I need something new."

"Enough, Divina!" Theodocus cried out. "This man does not deserve to die! Let him go and return me to my torment."

"Oh, I will return you to your torment. You can be certain of that," Divina purred. "But perhaps you are right. A quick death would be boring. I propose a challenge. But first, you must tell me your name, warrior."

"They call me Jack," the samurai replied.

"Not much of a name for a warrior," Divina sneered. "But no matter. My offer of a challenge still stands. You will perform six tasks of my choosing. If you complete them all, I will give you your freedom."

"And if I refuse?" Jack asked.

Divina's face became a mask of anger. Green light flashed in the temple, and Jack suddenly found himself back on the hillside, chained to the boulder. His hands and feet were clamped tightly inside metal rings.

Divina's voice boomed all around him. "If you refuse, I will see that you remain chained here for eternity!"

Green light flashed again, and Jack found himself back in the temple.

"Well," Divina asked, "what will you choose?"

"I will accept your challenge," Jack said. By accepting Divina's challenge, there was at least some hope that he would survive. "But if I succeed, you must let Theodocus go free as well."

Divina considered this. "Very well," she said. "I suppose you would only try to free Theo again. But he must accompany you on your tasks."

Jack turned to Theo. The man's pale blue eyes were filled with panic. "We cannot trust her," he whispered.

"Is there another way?" Jack asked.

Theodocus shook his head.

Jack took a step toward Divina. "We will accept your challenge," he said calmly.

"I knew you would," Divina said. "Let's see . . . which

task shall I give you first? It should be difficult, but not too difficult. It would be terribly boring if you failed on the first try."

A light flickered in Divina's eyes. "That's it!" she said. "For your first task, you must destroy the hydra."

Theodocus turned pale. "No," he said, his voice pleading. "Not the hydra!"

The hydra? Jack wondered. *What is a hydra?*

Green light flashed, and Jack felt himself being torn out of the temple again. This time, he and Theo landed in a cool, dark cave. Jack guessed that the cave's opening was right behind them, because pale yellow sunlight streamed in, illuminating the cave's interior.

The light shone on some kind of huge creature sleeping against the cave wall. It had a long tail like a dragon's, shiny green scales, and nine heads, each one attached to a long neck. Each head had a snarling snout filled with sharp white fangs.

"The hydra!" Theo cried.

At the sound of Theo's voice, all nine heads snapped awake. Each one let out a cry that sounded like a cross between a lion's roar and a raven's screech. The deafening sound bounced against the cave walls.

"Go!" Jack told Theodocus. "I will handle this."

Theodocus started to run out of the cave, then stopped.

"But Jack," he said. "There's something you need to know about the —"

His voice was drowned out by the cry of the hydra as it leaped to its feet and charged at Jack. He could feel heat radiating from the hydra's closest head as it jerked toward him, trying to take a bite out of his shoulder.

Jack's sword gleamed as he swung it in a perfect circle, cleanly slicing through the neck. The head clattered to the floor of the cave. Liquid trickled out of the neck and sizzled as it hit the earth. Jack noticed a familiar spark of electricity and some frayed wires.

So. The hydra was another robot.

I can do this, Jack thought. *Just eight more to go.*

The hydra's remaining eight heads roared again. For a moment, it seemed paralyzed by anger. Jack used the time to take a few steps backward toward the cave entrance. Fighting the hydra would be easier out in the open.

But then the hydra's cry was replaced by another sound — the sound of groaning metal. Small white sparks shot out from the severed neck. Jack watched in amazement as green metal scales snaked out, forming a new head.

Before a minute had passed, the new head was complete. It opened its jaws and joined the other heads in a victory cry.

"That's what I was trying to tell you," Theodocus said from behind him. "When you cut off one of the hydra's heads, another grows to replace it."

"Is there anything else I should know?" Jack asked.

"Yes," Theo said. "The hydra's bite is poisonous. If its teeth break your skin, you will die."

Before Jack had time to think, the hydra charged forward once again. All nine heads angrily snapped their teeth.

"Theo, get back!" Jack called out.

Theo did not need to be told twice. He ran and took shelter behind a nearby rock. Jack was grateful. He needed room to maneuver.

Another head jerked toward Jack with its mouth wide open. Jack swung his sword again. With one swift movement he chopped off the head. And just like before, a new head formed in its place seconds later.

Jack circled the hydra, weighing his options. Cutting off heads was no use, he knew, but it would keep him safe for awhile. And Jack would not tire out any time soon. He'd have to keep fighting until he thought of some way to destroy the hydra. Everything had a weakness. He just had to find it.

Jack darted around the hydra, moving this way and that, hoping to confuse the creature. But confusing nine heads wasn't easy. One by one, the heads lurched at Jack, their sharp teeth flashing.

One by one, Jack sliced off their heads.

The smell of electricity and burnt metal filled the air, along with a foul smell Jack guessed was poison. A thick black liquid leaked from the severed necks, forming small puddles on the ground. Now Jack had to avoid stepping in them, too.

Jack swung his sword again and again. It was becoming harder and harder to think of a plan when he was facing hungry heads at every turn.

"Jack, there's something strange about this," Theo said.

Swish! Jack sliced off another head. What was Theo saying?

"The ninth head! The one in the center," Theo called out. "It has not attacked you."

Swish! Jack swung his sword again as Theo's words registered. He was right. The head in the center of the hydra did not snake out, searching, like the others. It was almost like the eight heads were protecting it.

And that's when Jack knew what to do.

"Its power must be stored there!" Jack called back. "I must destroy it!"

There was only one way. With a cry, Jack jumped up above the hydra, somersaulting through the air. He landed lightly on the hydra's back, right behind the ninth head.

There was no time to waste. Jack raised his sword with both hands, then thrust down with all his might. The sword pierced the hydra's metal skull. Jack quickly let go and jumped off of the hydra's back.

For one horrifying moment, the hydra screamed as though it was possessed with new energy. But it was only a last gasp. The screams stopped all at once, and the hydra collapsed to the ground.

Jack carefully stepped around the puddles of poison and retrieved his sword. Theo came running out from behind the rock.

"Thank you," Jack said. "Your observation was indeed a wise one."

"You are amazing!" Theo said, grabbing Jack's hand. "Stranger, what is your story?"

But there was no time for talk. Divina's face appeared

before them. She was smiling, but it wasn't a very happy smile.

"Your sword has done you well, Jack," she said. "But you cannot always depend on it. For your next task, you must clean the Stables of Agnes before the sun rises tomorrow. Follow the river — and the stench."

Then Divina disappeared.

"The Stables of Agnes?" Jack asked Theo.

"Agnes is the wealthiest person in Mythologia," Theo explained. "She rents her land out to the poor, and takes their cattle when they can't pay her high prices. She has more than one thousand cattle in her stables, yet she has never cleaned them."

"I see," Jack said. A thousand cattle? Divina's newest task sounded impossible. But he had to try.

Jack and Theo followed Divina's instructions and walked along the riverbank. They stopped for a brief rest while Theo drank deeply from the river and gathered some berries and nuts to eat. When they continued, Jack found time to tell Theo of his mission to destroy Aku.

"And now, my friend," Jack said, "tell me how you came to be chained to that rock."

But before Theo could answer, a rushing, roaring sound filled their ears. The river began to swirl violently.

And then a figure rose up out of the water. A huge man towered above them, blocking the sun.

"I am Reginald the River Giant," said the man in a booming voice. "Do not take another step!"

Jack looked up at the giant. "Please let us pass," he said. "There is something we must do."

Reginald stomped his foot down into the river. A big wave washed up on shore, drenching Jack and Theo.

"Everybody is always in such a hurry!" the giant complained. "Nobody ever wants to stay and talk to me. Ever since my brother Ronald went to live in the plains, I have been so lonely."

"We're sorry!" Theo called up. "We are on a mission from Divina. If we don't complete it, it will be the end of us both."

The giant stomped his foot again. Another wave splashed out of the river. Jack dodged out of the way in time, but Theo got soaked again.

"Divina Divina Divina!" roared the giant. "She's always spoiling everything."

"Then you understand?" Theo called up.

Reginald grinned. "Oh, I understand, all right. Since Divina is going to destroy you anyway, you might as well stay here and have fun with me!"

The giant bent down and swiped at Theo with his large, fleshy hand. Jack grabbed Theo by the arm and pulled him away just in time.

Startled, Reginald lost his balance. He toppled over, landing in the river with a loud crash. Jack pulled Theo along without looking back.

"Slow down, Jack!" Theo said, panting. "I can't keep up!"

Jack looked back at the riverbank. Reginald was sitting up, rubbing his head. He didn't seem concerned about following them.

That was just fine with Jack. They had enough to worry about without an angry giant getting involved.

"Fine," Jack said. "Now, how do we find this Agnes?"

Theo stopped, sniffing the air. "Divina was speaking the truth when she said to follow the stench."

Jack realized Theo was right. As they walked down the river, a terrible smell in the air got stronger and stronger.

Jack had smelled some bad things in his travels. But this was worse than all of them. Worse than a hundred sweaty Himalayan yaks. Even worse than the stench of evil that surrounded Aku, if that was possible.

Jack scanned the riverbank for a plant that might help. Finally, he saw some bushy rosemary growing on a slope. He picked a stalk of the clean-smelling herb and held it to his nose. He gave one to Theo as well.

The herb helped for a few minutes, but not much longer. By the time the smell became unbearable again, the stables were in view.

Jack and Theo stopped, stunned by the sight. The stables looked as though they stretched out for a mile. Inside the rickety wooden walls and fences, hundreds of cattle milled about — where they could find room. Tons of manure covered every spare inch.

Almost as bad as the smell was the noise of thousands, maybe millions of buzzing black flies that hovered over the whole mess. Jack had never seen anything like it.

"Curse you, Divina," Theo muttered under his breath. "I will be the end of you, I swear it."

Jack did not respond. He was busy thinking of a way — any way — to get these stables clean. Just then, a woman approached them.

The woman's black hair was piled high on her head. She wore a purple toga and was smiling as though she was walking through a rose garden instead of past the hideous stables.

"You must be Agnes," Jack said.

"Why yes," she said, revealing large white teeth. "And what brings you two handsome gentlemen here?"

"Divina sent us," Theo explained. "To clean your stables."

Agnes raised an eyebrow. "Why would my stables need to be cleaned? Things are just fine the way they are."

Jack was not surprised by Agnes's remark. Nothing in Aku's strange world really surprised him anymore.

Theo, on the other hand, was astounded.

"'Just fine'? Can't you *smell* it?" he asked.

Agnes shrugged. "You get used to it. It beats paying someone to keep them clean. The pleasure I get from my riches far outweighs the stench."

"Well, it doesn't matter," Theo said. "Because we've got to clean it. Divina's orders."

Agnes scowled. "Don't expect me to pay you. Or feed you while you're staying here. That's Divina's problem."

"We won't be here long," Theo replied. "We've got to get this done before sunrise."

Agnes laughed. It reminded Jack of the howler monkeys he had heard while traveling through the jungle.

"That's funny. Divina must be toying with you," Agnes said. "In that case, I think I'll stay and watch."

Agnes walked to a nearby tree and sat down in the shade. She looked at Jack and Theo expectantly.

"Go on," she said. "I think there are shovels down there somewhere."

The mounds of manure stretched out as far as Jack could see. Even if he and Theo could manage to shovel it all, it would take weeks, maybe months.

Theo was thinking the same thing. "It will take an ocean to clean out this mess," he said.

Something clicked in Jack's head. "Or a river!" he said. "If only there was some way to harness the river's water . . ."

"Maybe Reginald would help us," Theo said. Then he grabbed Jack's arm. "That's it! All we have to do is make Reginald angry. He'll stomp his feet, and the river will overflow into the stables."

Jack considered this. It sounded far-fetched. But right now, there seemed to be no other solution.

"Let us try it," Jack said. He and Theo headed back down the river.

"Hey, where are you going?" Agnes screeched.

"We'll be back!" Theo promised.

Jack and Theo did not have to go far. Reginald was walking down the river, looking toward them.

"Hey!" Reginald called out when he saw them. "Did you come back to play with me?"

"No!" Theo yelled. "Who would want to play with a big monster like you?"

"That's not nice!" Reginald roared, stomping his feet again.

"We must get closer to the stables," Jack told Theo. "Run!"

They ran back toward the stables with Reginald at their heels.

"Are we playing hide-and-seek?" Reginald wondered, stomping through the water.

Soon they came to the point where the river ran closest to the stables. Jack and Theo stopped.

"Now," Jack said, "make him angry again."

"You're so big you could use the ocean for a bathtub!" Theo called out. "You're so big you could use the Colosseum for a drinking cup!"

Reginald began to stomp his feet. Water sloshed out of the river and trickled toward the stables.

"We need more," Theo said. "You try, Jack."

Jack hesitated. "Well, I —"

"Come on, Jack," Theo prodded.

Jack cleared his throat. "Oh, giant!" he yelled. "You are . . . you are definitely an unusually large size!"

Reginald stopped, puzzled.

"I guess I should do this one myself," Theo said. He yelled up at Reginald. "Jack meant to say that you're a big boring baby and nobody wants to play with you!"

That did it. Reginald exploded into a full-fledged tantrum. He stomped his feet. He pounded the water with his fists.

Behind him, a tidal wave of river water began to form. Jack began to think Theo's plan might work.

Then he remembered — the cattle!

"I must free them," he told Theo. "Get to a high place as soon as you can!"

Jack ran as fast as he could toward the stables. One by one he opened the gates. The cattle didn't hesitate. They ran out, scattering into the fields beyond.

"Hey, you can't do that!" Agnes shrieked. "I'll make you so miserable that you'll never —"

But a wave of river water knocked Agnes backward as it cascaded toward the stables. Jack grabbed her and carried her into the branches of a tree. Theo was already

waiting there for him.

The water raced through the stables, pushing out the filth. By the time Reginald's temper tantrum ended, they were clean. Only the fresh smell of water remained.

"Somebody is going to pay for this!" Agnes complained.

"Talk to Divina," Theo said.

Suddenly, Divina's green face flashed in the sky in front of them. "I am here," she said, with anger in her voice. "And it is time for your next task!"

5

"I think I have been too easy on you," Divina said. "You have completed the first two tasks with much less trouble than I anticipated. I'll have to think carefully before naming your next challenge."

Theo jumped down from the tree.

"Easy?" he yelled. "The hydra's poison — not to mention the stench from the stables — almost killed us!"

Jack jumped down next to Theo and put a steadying hand on his shoulder. At first Jack thought the man he had rescued was timid and weak. But he seemed to be regaining his strength — and his courage.

Jack looked into Divina's eyes.

"Name your challenge, then," he said calmly.

"Very well," Divina replied. "You shall silence the Symphonium Birds!"

Theo muttered something under his breath as Divina disappeared. Jack guessed that what lay ahead of them wasn't easy, but there was no use protesting. Unless he could figure out a way to fight Divina, he would end up chained to a rock, just like Theo. At least this way he stood a chance.

"Symphonium is about a day's journey away," Theo said, wringing water out of his cloak. "I don't see why Divina couldn't just have taken us there."

"Perhaps she wants us to tire out," Jack said. "But I think we are fortunate. We can rest overnight. And now you will have time to tell me about Divina."

The sun was setting as Jack and Theo began their journey. Theo explained his story as he walked.

"For as long as the people of Mythologia can remember, Divina has been our leader," Theo said. "She is all-powerful. She controls the lives of everyone who lives here, and she is not kind. For ages, we have lived in terror.

"Divina had always told us that she was immortal, indestructible," Theo continued. "But some of us held a hope that there was a way to destroy her. We began to investigate. Divina found out. The others escaped, but I stayed behind. Someone has to fight for my people."

Jack nodded in understanding. Theo must have had great courage to stay and fight instead of run.

"That is when I became chained to the rock as punishment for my crime," Theo said. "To be honest, I had given up all hope. Until you came along. You have given me back my life — and my courage."

"Our fight is not over yet," Jack said. "What do you know of these Symphonium Birds?"

"They live on a cliff on the border of Mythologia," Theo explained. "It is said that anyone who hears their song will turn to stone. I'm surprised that Divina wants them silenced. They have served her cruel purpose many times."

"She must believe we will fail," Jack said.

"She may be right," Theo said. "I do not see how we can succeed."

After the sun set, they set up camp in a quiet clearing. Theo built a fire, and they gathered a few berries and nuts to eat.

Suddenly, Jack heard the sound of a twig snapping behind him. He turned toward the noise.

An old woman walked out of the trees. She wore a dark hooded robe. Her gray hair was braided and piled on top of her head.

"Please, kind strangers," the woman said. "Can you spare some food for an old woman?"

Jack only hesitated for a brief second. This woman could be a threat in disguise, but she looked more hungry than dangerous. He gladly gave her his berries and nuts. He had gone without food before.

Theo looked at his food wistfully, but gave it to the woman just the same.

"Here, good woman," he said. "Would you like to warm yourself by our fire?"

The woman held the food in both hands. A slow smile appeared on her face. In an instant, the berries and nuts vanished. In its place were two new red berries and one white one.

"Your kindness shall be repaid," she said, dropping the three berries into Jack's hand. "I know of

your quest. When you reach the trio of tall pines, you must each eat a red berry. You will be safe from the sound of the Symphonium Birds, but only for a short time."

"But how can we silence them?" Theo asked her.

"Use the white berry," she replied. "One bird is not like the others. Feed the white berry to that bird, and the song of the birds will be silenced forever."

"Thank you," Jack said. The woman disappeared into the dark night as quickly as she had come.

"It is said that the forests of Mythologia are inhabited by spirits," Theo said in a whisper. "I always thought they were dangerous."

Jack looked at the berries in his hand. He was not sure if the woman — or spirit — could be trusted, but instinct told him she was not part of Divina's plan.

Jack and Theo woke before sunrise and continued walking. By early afternoon a tall cliff came into view in the distance. They stopped inside a circle of three tall pine trees.

"We must be careful," Theo said. "If we get close enough to hear the song of the birds, we will be turned to stone."

Jack examined their surroundings. The three pines must be the "trio of tall pines" the old woman had told them about. But what lay beyond?

Jack looked down the trail that led to the cliff. He saw rocks, trees — and something else. Theo saw it, too.

"Are those statues?" Theo asked.

Tall stone figures jutted up from the trail less than a half mile ahead. They could have been statues.

"Or men turned to stone," Jack said. "These trees must mark the last safe point before the sound of the birds can be heard."

Jack took the two red berries from the pouch he wore around his belt. Theo looked at the berries, looked at Jack, and nodded.

"We have nothing to lose," Theo said.

They each took a berry and ate it. Jack did not feel any different.

Then he noticed Theo's mouth moving — but Jack could hear no words.

In fact, Jack realized, he could hear nothing at all. The woman had told the truth. But she had also said the effect of the berries would not last for long.

Jack saw from Theo's expression that he had realized the same thing. The two began to run down the trail.

Soon they passed the stone figures they had seen from the trees. Up close, they were disturbing. The faces of the men were frozen in expressions of shock and agony. Many held their hands to their ears. Jack could only imagine what hideous music the birds made.

They reached the bottom of the hill. A trail led up to the cliff's edge. It was a steep and rocky climb. Jack made his way up as swiftly as a mountain goat, but he could see Theo struggling behind him. Jack got to the top first and waited for his friend.

Cautiously, Jack led the way to the cliff's edge. He and Theo hid behind a rock and peered over the cliff's edge.

Hundreds, maybe thousands of birds roosted in the rocky crags of the cliffs. The birds looked like crows. Their shiny black feathers gleamed with a deep purple sheen. The birds' mouths were open, and Jack knew they were singing their paralyzing song.

Jack scanned the birds. The old woman had said that one bird was different. But as far as Jack could see, every bird looked alike. He wondered how much time they had.

Next to him, Theo jumped up and pointed at something. Theo's mouth was open, as though he was shouting. Jack couldn't hear it, of course.

But the birds could. In one moment, thousands of beady black eyes all turned in their direction. In the next instant, the birds took off from the cliff side and zoomed toward them.

Jack grabbed Theo and started to run. But the birds were too fast. Jack felt a bird's sharp claws as it landed on his head. Another landed on his arm. Three more on his back.

They were being attacked — and there was no escape!

Jack fought off the birds as they pecked at his skin with their sharp beaks. The birds did not weigh much, and Jack could have easily fought off one, or ten, or even twenty. But hundreds of birds joined the attack.

Jack ran across the hilltop, searching for shelter. He pulled Theo along until they came to a small pond. It would have to do. Jack jumped in, dragging Theo with him. The birds would not follow them under the water.

Holding his breath, Jack looked up out of the water. The black figures of the angry birds looked like a cloud blocking the sky.

And then, suddenly, he saw a flash of white.

One bird is not like the others, the woman had said. Could this be the one?

Jack saw from Theo's expression that his friend could not hold his breath any longer. Theo swam to the water's surface, and the birds enveloped him. Jack would have to move fast.

Jack did not take his eyes off of the white flash. From its movement, Jack knew it was definitely a bird. This was it. He gripped the white berry in his hand.

He waited until just the right moment and then shot out of the water like a rocket. Birds swarmed around him, but Jack was moving too fast. With one hand, he grabbed the white bird. With the other, he threw the berry down the bird's open beak. Then he closed the beak, forcing the berry down the bird's gullet.

All at once the birds stopped moving. They flew to the ground and looked at each other in confusion. Jack could see that they were opening their mouths to cry out. But had the berry silenced them?

And then he heard Theo's voice.

"Well did it work or not?" Theo asked.

Jack looked at his friend. Theo's face and arms were cov-

ered in scratches. His cloak dripped with pond water. But he had heard Theo speak. And he had not heard the birds.

"You and I can hear again," Jack said. "And since we cannot hear the birds, then we must have succeeded."

"Curse those forest spirits!" Divina complained, her face appearing in the sky above them. "I should burn down the forest once and for all."

"Do not take out your anger on the forest," Theo pleaded. "Please, give us our fourth task. That should entertain you for awhile."

"I suppose you are right," Divina replied. "I should not waste my time with other pleasures when I only have three more chances to see you fail."

"So what will it be?" Theo asked.

"Fetch me the Singing Giraffe of Thena," Divina said. "I could use some amusement. Ronald the Giant has been enjoying its song for too long."

"Hey, that must be Reginald's brother," Theo whispered to Jack. But the samurai had another concern.

"You are asking me to steal," Jack said. "That is something I will not do."

"It is not my concern how you get the giraffe," Divina snapped. "Just get it!" Then she vanished.

Theo sat down on the grass. "I hate how she toys with us!" he cried, shaking his fist at the sky. "If she wants the Singing Giraffe, why doesn't she just get it herself?"

"Perhaps it is for the same reason she did not transport us again," Jack said. "Her powers may be limited by distance."

Theo scratched his head. "You know, you might be right. It is rare for her to appear outside her temple. Maybe her power gets weaker if she travels from it."

Theo stood up and grabbed Jack by the sleeve of his robe. "Jack, we could run! We could run and she wouldn't be able to hurt us!"

"We do not know for sure," Jack said. "I made a bargain with Divina. I will not break my word."

"But she's evil, Jack!" Theo said. "You can't bargain with someone who's evil!"

Jack knew that what Theo said made sense. But he was beginning to form a plan of his own. Divina might be useful to him.

"Run if you choose," he told Theo. "I will understand. But this is my choice."

Theo sighed. "I'm not going anywhere — except to find the Singing Giraffe! Reginald said his brother Ronald went to live in the plains. They are not far."

Theo led Jack back down the cliff. The two men walked for hours in the afternoon sun. They passed an orchard along the way, and were able to fill their stomachs with apples and water from a cold spring.

The sun was just starting to sink in the sky when they came to a large, flat expanse of land. The land was desolate except for a few tall trees here and there.

"These are the plains," Theo said. "But where is Ronald? It shouldn't be hard to spot a giant and a giraffe."

Jack and Theo walked on for another hour. Soon Jack picked up a peculiar sound. As they walked closer to the noise, Jack realized it was the sound of singing.

"Oh, it's nice to live here in the plains. Except that it almost never rains. It's so dry and dusty, my hair is all musty, my hooves are all rusty . . ."

The song was loud and badly out of tune.

"It must be the Singing Giraffe," Theo exclaimed, and soon they saw he was right. A giraffe stood next to a tree, stretching its long neck toward the sky and singing. At the foot of the tree sat a giant who looked very much like Reginald. Except this giant held his hands to his ears and wore an expression of pain on his face.

"What should we do?" Theo whispered. "Do you want to attack him?"

"This giant has done nothing to hurt us," Jack replied. "And I wlll not steal from him. We should try to talk to him."

"Oh, right," Theo said. "Because we all know how friendly and helpful giants are. I'm sure he'll just say, 'Go ahead, take my giraffe!'"

Theo was still talking as Jack stepped toward the giant. He gently tapped him on the ankle.

"Excuse me," Jack said. He

had to raise his voice to be heard above the giraffe. "May I talk with you?"

"Will you please be quiet?" Ronald bellowed. At first Jack thought he was talking to him, but the giant looked up at the giraffe. The giraffe kept singing.

Ronald scooped up Jack in his palm and brought Jack up to his face.

"Sorry," Ronald said. "It's the only way I can hear you. What is it you wanted?"

"We have been sent on a quest from Divina," Jack said. "She wants us to bring her your giraffe."

Ronald was silent for a second, and then he tilted back his head and let out a roar. Jack reached for his sword, prepared to defend himself.

But then he realized that Ronald wasn't angry. He was laughing.

"Go ahead!" Ronald boomed. "Take my giraffe! Please!"

7

"Thank you," Jack said. The giant lowered him back to the ground.

But Theo looked stunned. "Wait a second!" he yelled up to Ronald. "You mean we can just take the Singing Giraffe of Thena? Just like that? What's the catch?"

Ronald leaned down. "The catch is, I will finally get some peace and quiet!" he bellowed. His breath knocked Theo off his feet. "I came all the way to the plains to escape this annoying creature, but it won't leave me alone!"

"Oh how I love to sing. I love it more than anything. I sing day and night in the dark and the light . . ."

"But the Singing Giraffe is legendary," Theo said, rising to his feet. "The tales say that kings have fought over it."

"I'm not surprised," Ronald said. "They probably fought over who would have to keep it! The creature never stops singing. It's a nightmare."

"Do you think it will come with us?" Jack asked.

"I hope so," Ronald said. He turned to the giraffe. "Hey, these guys want to take you to Divina. You'll have a new crowd to try out your material on. What do you say?"

"A journey would be very nice. I've been round the world once or twice. As long as it's clean and Divina's not mean . . ."

"I'll take that as a yes," Ronald interrupted. "Now, please get out of here, all of you! I need some sleep."

Jack and Theo led the giraffe back to the edge of the plain. There was no sign of Divina until they reached the apple orchard. Then her face appeared above the trees.

"So you have succeeded once again," Divina said. "But your next task will not be so simple. I want you to bring me three golden lemons from the Isle of Citrus."

Divina's face began to fade away again.

"Hey, wait!" Theo yelled. "What about the giraffe?"

"You can bring him to my temple when your quest is finished," she said, and she was gone.

"Oh, I like apples. I like apples. Yes I do. Yes I do. Red ones, yellow ones, green ones, spotted ones . . ."

The giraffe cheerfully continued singing, completely undisturbed by the fact that a giant green head had just appeared before them.

By now the sky had turned black and was dotted with stars. "We should probably camp here," Theo said. He looked at the giraffe. "I wonder if it sings in its sleep?"

In response, the giraffe started to sing a lullaby. "Let's all go to sleep sleep sleep. Let's all sleep so deep deep deep . . ."

The giraffe sang the lullaby in a low, sweet voice. Jack

and Theo found themselves drifting off into peaceful slumber. But as soon as the first rays of the sun began to dawn, the song changed again — and the giraffe's voice was loud and off-key once more.

"Wake up! It's a brand-new day! Wake up! Now it's time to play! Wake up! . . ."

Theo groaned. "You know, being chained to that rock wasn't so bad after all."

Jack smiled. Thanks to his samurai training, he was able to tune out the giraffe and concentrate on his journey. But he knew things weren't so easy for Theo.

After a breakfast of apples and water, the trio set out to find the golden lemons.

"The Isle of Citrus isn't really an island," Theo explained as they walked. "It's a rock just off the shore by the sea. Golden lemons grow from a single tree on the rock. It is said that anyone who eats the lemons will enjoy good health for as long as they live."

Jack pondered this. Fetching lemons off of a tree sounded simple enough. But he knew there had to be a catch. He'd just have to wait to find out what it was.

They traveled all day, and found a small clearing in

which to spend the night. They had walked a short distance the next morning when Jack smelled salt in the air.

"The sea," Theo said. "I smell it, too."

Soon they were walking toward the water's edge. The giraffe began to sing again.

"Oh, how I love the sea! A sailor's life for me! I'll see fish and whales and boats with sails . . ."

Jack peered out over the water. In the distance, a tall black rock jutted out of the waves. Atop the rock was a short green tree. Its branches glittered in the sunlight.

"It's the golden lemons!" Theo said excitedly. "How are we going to get there?"

Jack watched the waves crash against the rock, leaving trails of churned-up foam as they retreated. He knew he could swim those waves, but what about Theo? He didn't want to be distracted by worry for his friend.

"I will go alone," Jack said. "Wait here."

Theo didn't argue. "Hey, Jack, bring back a few extra lemons while you're at it, okay?"

Jack took off his robe and walked into the sea. As soon as it was deep enough, he dove in. The icy cold water seemed to seep into his bones.

But Jack didn't mind the chill — it energized him. Fighting against the current, he used strong strokes to swim toward the rock.

Soon the slick black rock was within reach. Jack circled, waiting for a moment of calm to make his approach.

Suddenly, the water began to churn. Jack felt his body begin to rise higher and higher.

"Raaaaaaaaaaaaawr!"

A huge head rose out of the water. The head was attached to a long body that curled like a snake's — except it was as wide as a tree trunk. A row of triangular fins spiked up from its neck. Two angry red eyes stared at Jack's face, and a long green tongue slid out from among rows of sharp white teeth.

"It's a sea serpent!" Theo cried.

8

Jack struggled to stay afloat as the sea serpent churned the water all around him. The monster was the only thing standing between him and the Isle of Citrus — and it didn't seem to be going anywhere.

So this is the catch, Jack thought. *There must be a way around it.*

But the sea serpent wasn't interested in giving Jack time to think. It lurched toward him, its red eyes blazing.

Jack dove underwater to escape the monster. He thought quickly. His sword was strapped to his side, as always, but it would not be easy to wield his weapon while being knocked about by the ocean waves. There had to be another way.

Jack swam to the surface. The sea serpent had its back to him. One look at the spiky fins gave Jack an idea.

Jack swam to the serpent and grabbed onto the end of its tail. The monster turned its head and shrieked in anger. It lashed its tail back and forth like a whip, trying to lose Jack.

But Jack held on. Little by little he made his way up the slippery tail. Then he grabbed onto the first fin and began to climb up the sea serpent's neck, moving up the fins one by one.

It was all Jack could do to hang on. The sea serpent bucked and lurched like a wild horse. The fins were slick and slippery with seawater.

But Jack did not let go. As the sea serpent moved closer and closer to the black rock, Jack got closer and closer to his goal.

Soon the tree of glittering lemons was almost in reach. Just a little higher, and Jack would be able to touch it.

But the sea serpent began to dive under the water. Jack dug the sharp heels of his sandals into the monster's neck. The creature reared up and let out an angry yell.

The moment only lasted a split second, but it was all Jack needed. He reached out and broke off a branch of the tree, quickly counting. There were five lemons — three for Divina with two to spare. Now all he had to do was get back to shore.

Jack clenched the branch in his teeth and dove into the water. He swam as fast as he could, but he could feel the serpent pushing through the water behind him.

Then a sharp pain shot through Jack's leg as something grabbed hold of his ankle. He felt his body being lifted out of the water. He twisted his head back to see that the sea serpent held him by his ankle in its mouth.

The monster began to swing its head back and forth, tossing Jack around like a rag doll. Jack's hands were free, so he plucked one lemon off of the branch and hurled it at the serpent's left eye.

Splat! The lemon hit its target. Golden juices squirted from the squashed fruit. The monster howled in pain as the juices seeped into its eye.

Jack dropped into the water when the sea serpent's mouth opened. But the creature still chased after him.

Jack took aim and threw another lemon at the monster's right eye. This one hit the spot, too, leaving the sea serpent temporarily blinded.

That was the break Jack needed. He swam to shore, ran onto the sand, and grabbed his robe.

"Jack! Do you have any lemons left?" Theo asked, worried.

"I have three," he replied. "But we must hurry. The creature may still pursue us."

The giraffe sang a new song as they hurried across the beach.

"Oh, this is the story of a man named Jack. He keeps his cool when monsters attack . . ."

They didn't stop until they were off the beach and had reached a dirt road.

"This road leads back to central Mythologia and Divina's temple," Theo said, after catching his breath. "I guess we should make our way there."

"Not without making one stop first!"

It was Divina. Her face glowered above them.

"You have one challenge left, lest you forget," she said. "And this one will not be so easy, you can be sure."

"I wouldn't call those other tasks easy," Theo said.

"Silence!" Divina boomed. "Your final task is at hand."

Green light flashed around them, and Jack realized they were being transported again. Theo had said they were close to Divina's temple. His theory about her power might be true.

But he did not have time to give that any more thought. He found himself transported to the floor of a large, open-air arena. Men and women in togas filled the seats. Theo and the giraffe were in a viewing box at the end of the arena.

Divina's face appeared in the center.

"Jack, meet your challenger," Divina said. "If you can beat my champion in a wrestling contest, your sixth task will be complete."

The crowd cheered. At the far end of the arena, a wooden gate swung open. Jack watched, ready for anything. Who would his challenger be?

Suddenly, a large, muscled bull stormed through the gate, snorting and puffing. It looked almost human. That might have been because it was wearing red pants.

The bull stopped just feet in front of Jack, stood on its back legs, and folded its arms across its chest.

"I am Taurus, Champion of Mythologia!" the bull roared. "No one can defeat me!"

9

Jack felt his sword vanish from his side. With relief, he saw it reappear next to Theo. That was fine. If this truly was a wrestling match, he would not need it.

Jack waited for some call or signal to begin the match, but Taurus was more impatient. He got back on all fours and charged after Jack. In the stands, the crowd cheered for their champion.

Jack somersaulted out of the way. Taurus was big, but he was also quick. Without missing a beat, he spun around and raced toward Jack again.

This time Jack reached out and grabbed the bull by the horns. If he was going to pin Taurus to the ground, he'd have to start somewhere.

Taurus hurled his muscled shoulders back, sending Jack flying.

Wham! Jack thudded onto the dirt. The blow had knocked the breath out of him. Taurus was not going to be easy to take down.

Jack jumped to his feet and tried another approach. Taurus charged at him again, and Jack jumped up and over the bull. Before landing, Jack spun around and grabbed Taurus's back legs.

Clouds of brown dust kicked up as Taurus skidded across the arena, dragging Jack behind him. Then Taurus stopped, stood upright, and proceeded to sit down.

Jack had no choice. He had to let go of the bull's legs or he'd be crushed by Taurus's massive weight.

Above them, Divina scowled. "Do not fail me, Taurus!" she cried.

A green light flashed in front of Taurus, and a long fighting stick appeared in his hooves.

"Hey, no fair!" Theo called out.

"This is a wrestling match," Divina snapped back. "Everything is fair!"

The fighting stick became a blur as Taurus twirled it in his front hooves. Then Taurus thrust the stick at Jack.

Whoosh! Whoosh! Whoosh!

Jack jumped and dodged. The stick never made contact. Angry, Taurus broke the stick in two and ran at Jack.

The match went on like this for hours. Jack tried every move he could think of to bring Taurus to his knees, but the bull would not go down. Taurus could not make contact with Jack, either, no matter how hard he tried.

The cheers of the crowd grew weaker and weaker as they slumped in their seats, bored and tired. Divina just seemed to get angrier and angrier.

Soon the sun had set, and the sky was a deep purple.

"If this match is not finished by the time the moon

rises over the stadium, I will declare a winner myself!"
Divina promised.

Jack knew what that meant. Divina would name Taurus as the winner, and all would be for nothing. He could not let that happen.

With a mighty cry, Jack charged at Taurus, aiming for the bull's side. He put all of his weight into the blow.

Wham! For the first time all day, Taurus was off his feet. Jack jumped onto his chest. All he had to do now was pin the bull's shoulders to the ground.

Taurus struggled underneath him. The bull was just too strong. Jack knew he would be on his feet again soon. But he had to try.

And then, another sound rose above the bull's grunts. It was the giraffe, singing his nighttime lullaby.

"Let's all go to sleep sleep sleep. Let's all sleep so deep deep deep . . ."

The song seemed to have a strange effect on Taurus. Jack felt the bull's muscles relax. His eyes began to flutter. The lullaby was putting him to sleep!

Jack acted quickly. He put all his weight on the bull's shoulders, pinning them to the dirt. The crowd cheered wildly.

Green light flashed in the stadium, taking the shape of angry lightning bolts. The arena shook as though stricken by an earthquake.

"No fair!" Divina wailed.

"This is wrestling!" Theo called back. "Everything is fair!"

"I suppose you have won," she said. "I will be true to my word, although it pains me to do so. Be gone, quickly, before I change my mind."

Theo grabbed Jack's sword, jumped out of the viewing box, and ran into the arena.

"We did it!" he cried. "Thank you, Jack!"

But Jack had not taken his eyes off of Divina. Now was

the time to put his plan into action. "Divina, wait!"

Divina looked curiously at Jack. "Are you sure you want to risk my anger? I may change my mind."

"I would like to make a deal with you," Jack said. "A gamble."

Divina raised an eyebrow. "A gamble? I like the sound of that. Go on."

"I have learned that you possess great power," Jack said. "I think your power can help me. I will accept one more challenge from you. If I succeed, then you will agree to help me. If I fail . . ."

"If you fail," Divina said, "then your punishment will be legendary!"

10

"I understand," Jack said. "But Theo will go free, no matter what happens."

"I suppose," Divina sighed. "Now tell me, what is it you want?"

"I want you to send me back to my own time," Jack said. "If you have the power to do that."

Divina laughed. "That will be child's play!" she said. "I should have guessed you were not of this world, warrior. Then it is agreed. Your challenge will be worthy of your request. You will bring me Cerebus, the three-headed dog that guards the Underworld."

"No!" Theo interrupted. "You can't do that to him. No one has ever faced that creature and lived."

"Your friend has chosen his fate," Divina said. "And now it begins!"

The ground shook under Jack's feet. A fissure opened up, and the samurai tumbled into the unknown.

As Jack fell, Theo tossed Jack's sword to him. Jack caught it in one hand. His body seemed to fall for ages, until finally he landed with a thud on a rocky surface.

A man in a white toga approached Jack. He was leafing through a book with a weathered leather cover.

"Another prisoner?" the man asked, visibly flustered. "Divina did not notify me of this."

"What is this place?" Jack asked.

The man peered at Jack over the top of his glasses. "Why, the Underworld, of course. Where Divina sends the prisoners of Mythologia."

Jack looked around. He was in a dark cavern. There was one tunnel in front of him, blocked by a gate, and another one behind.

"I am looking for Cerebus," Jack said.

The gatekeeper chuckled. "No one looks for Cerebus unless they are looking for death. You must be mad."

"Divina has sent me for Cerebus," Jack said.

The gatekeeper looked at Jack, thought for a minute, and then shrugged.

"If you want to face Cerebus, it's your doom," he said. "Who am I to stop you?" He took a key from his belt, walked to the gate, and opened it. "It's in there."

"Thank you," Jack said. He steadied his sword in front of him and stepped into the darkness.

Jack listened carefully for the sound of breathing, but he heard nothing. His first sign of Cerebus was six glowing red eyes.

No breath, Jack thought. *So it's another robot.* The samurai stayed still until his eyes adjusted to the dark tunnel. Then the form of the robot dog took shape. Its body was made of hard steel plates. Its long metal tail ended in a spike. The dog's three heads looked identical, with long snouts opened to reveal pointy metal teeth. And right now, all three heads were looking at Jack.

A low, hoarse growl rose up from the depths of the dog. Unlike Taurus, this opponent was in no hurry to attack. Jack could understand why. The narrow tunnel meant that Jack had only two choices: face the dog, or turn and run.

Jack held his sword out in front of him. He could not use his sword to destroy the dog, but the robot did not know that. It kept the creature at bay for a few moments.

But then the dog leaped, as Jack knew it would. Jack threw himself on the ground, flattening his body against the cold stone. The dog jumped right over him.

Jack jumped to his feet and took the few seconds he had to develop a plan. Every robot had a power source. That knowledge had helped him defeat the hydra. He just had to find a way to cut the dog's power temporarily so he could take it back to Divina.

But Cerebus's power source was not obvious, and Jack had no more time to look. The angry dog pounced again.

Jack jumped up and swung his sword — but not at the robot. Instead, he sliced through a hard stone stalactite hanging from the tunnel's ceiling. The sharp stone pounded into Cerebus, landing on its back.

Cerebus howled, but did not appear to be damaged. It swiped at Jack with its right front leg. Sharp metal claws tore through Jack's robes as he jumped up again, slicing another stalactite.

This one collided with Cerebus's left head. The red lights in the eyes faded to black.

Jack grunted with satisfaction. The blow had short-circuited the power to one of the dog's heads. He just had to finish off the other two.

Jack jumped in the air again. His sword moved like lightning as it sheared stone after stone from the ceiling.

At the same time, Cerebus tackled Jack, pinning him to the floor. Jack was helpless, his arms pinned firmly at his sides. Two robot heads pushed toward his face, snapping rows of sharp teeth . . .

Whack! Whack! Two falling stalactites hit their marks just in time. The remaining two heads lost power, thudding into Jack's chest.

Jack used all of his strength to push the robot dog off his body. Then he grabbed the dog by the tail and dragged it down the tunnel.

The gatekeeper's face blanched when he saw Jack emerge from the tunnel with the defeated dog.

"How do I return to Divina's temple?" Jack asked him.

The gatekeeper pointed to the other opening. Jack nodded his thanks and entered the second tunnel.

He didn't get far when the tunnel was flooded with green light. As the light faded, Jack found himself inside

Divina's white marble temple. Divina's face floated there. Theo and the Singing Giraffe stood next to her.

"Jack!" Theo said, grinning. "I had to see if you were all right. I can't believe it."

Even Divina looked at Jack with grudging respect.

"Are you sure you want to go back in time, Jack?" she asked. "You could rule Mythologia here with me."

"Thank you," Jack said. "But I must return home. It is my destiny."

"Very well," Divina said. A soft green glow began to fill the temple. "You shall have your wish."

"I'll miss you, Jack," Theo said sadly.

Thoughts crowded Jack's head as the green glow grew brighter. He had been through so much in this evil world of Aku's. Could it be that his journey had finally ended? Was he really going back home?

And, as if in a nightmare, a familiar voice answered Jack's thoughts.

"Sorry, Samurai. You will not be going home today!"

"Aku!" Jack cried.

11

The demon seemed to fill the temple with his evil presence. Jack knew Aku's hideous features all too well. Red flames leaped from his eyes and cascaded under his chin. Sharp white teeth gleamed in Aku's bright green face.

Jack expected Aku to attack him. But instead, he turned his attention to Divina.

"I hate to do this, Divina," Aku said. "You have been quite useful to me, keeping the citizens of Mythologia in a state of eternal fear. But I never dreamed your powers could be used to help my enemy."

Divina looked panicked. "Your enemy? But Aku, I had no idea. Please —"

Her pleading was cut off by a loud rumbling sound.

The temple began to shake violently. Jack lost his footing as the marble broke apart beneath him. He knocked into Theo, and they slid across the floor.

As Jack rose to his feet, he realized the source of Divina's panic. The broken floor revealed a huge supercomputer of some kind.

"The source of Divina's power!" Theo cried. "It makes sense. It must be why her powers are strongest here at the temple."

Divina aimed a blast of green light at Aku, but the demon only laughed.

"I created you, Divina!" he cackled. "You cannot destroy me!"

Then red fire shot from Aku's eyes, zapping the giant computer. Metal melted, wires sizzled, and Divina let out one last scream before her face faded into nothing.

Rage and pain welled up inside Jack. He had been so close.

"Aku!" he cried, flying across the room with his sword raised.

But Aku had only come to destroy Divina — not to

74

fight Jack. The demon was powerful, yet he could not defend himself against Jack's sword, and he knew it.

"Good-bye, Samurai!" Aku laughed. "I hope you have learned your lesson. There is no way you can win!"

And then he vanished.

Jack stood motionless. The disappointment was almost too much to bear.

Then he felt a hand on his shoulder. Theo.

"Don't listen to him, Jack," he said. "A few days ago I was chained to a rock. I had lost all hope. But you showed me that life could be different, Jack. Think of all the things we have done together these last few days. Anything is possible, Jack!"

Jack nodded. "I will not give up," he said. "But what will you do? What will your people do now that Divina is gone?"

"Celebrate, I expect," Theo said. "It's about time we learned how to govern our own lives."

"That is good," Jack said. "And now I will be on my way."

"Not so fast," Theo said. "I know a great place to eat not far from here. You saved my life. At least I owe you a meal."

"I would be honored," Jack said.

"Oh, I like to eat. Some food is sweet. Some food is not.

Instead It's hot. But I'll eat it anyway because . . ."

The Singing Giraffe sauntered up to them, carefully stepping over piles of broken marble.

"What will you do with him?" Jack asked.

Theo shrugged. "I don't know. He kind of grows on you, don't you think?"

Jack smiled. Maybe Theo was right. If Theo could get used to the Singing Giraffe, then maybe anything was possible.

There is a way I can win, Aku, Jack thought. *And I will find it, I promise you!*

Superpowers or Superbrains?
Who Would Win in the Ultimate Cartoon Cookoff?

You decide. Pick up new Kid Cuisine® meals featuring Dexter and The Powerpuff Girls®, then vote for your favorite Cartoon Cook at CartoonNetwork.com/KCCookoff, and get exclusive Cartoon Orbit cToons!

CARTOON NETWORK™

CARTOON ORBIT®